*For our Paul*

# Little Red

## A FIZZINGLY GOOD YARN

RETOLD BY LYNN ROBERTS
ILLUSTRATED BY DAVID ROBERTS

Harry N. Abrams, Inc., Publishers

I n a time not too long ago and in a land much like our own, there lived a young boy. His name was Thomas, but—for some reason—everyone called him Little Red.

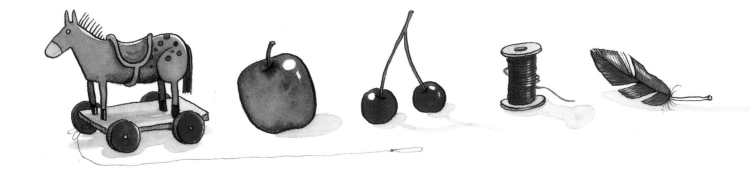

Little Red's parents owned a cozy inn, and people came from far and wide for a glass of their famous sweet ginger ale. Little Red loved to meet the travelers and hear their tales of dangerous encounters with dashing highwaymen and fearsome wolves.

One day Little Red was getting ready to visit his grandma, as he did every week, with a basketful of delicious treats and a week's supply of ginger ale.

"Grandma's favorite," declared Little Red, as he put the keg of ginger ale in his basket.

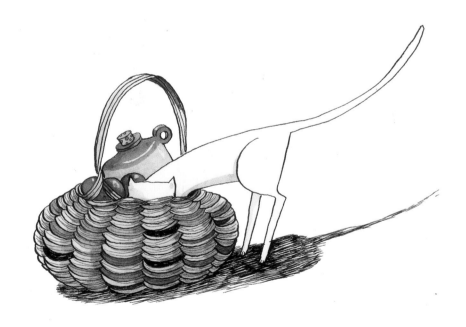

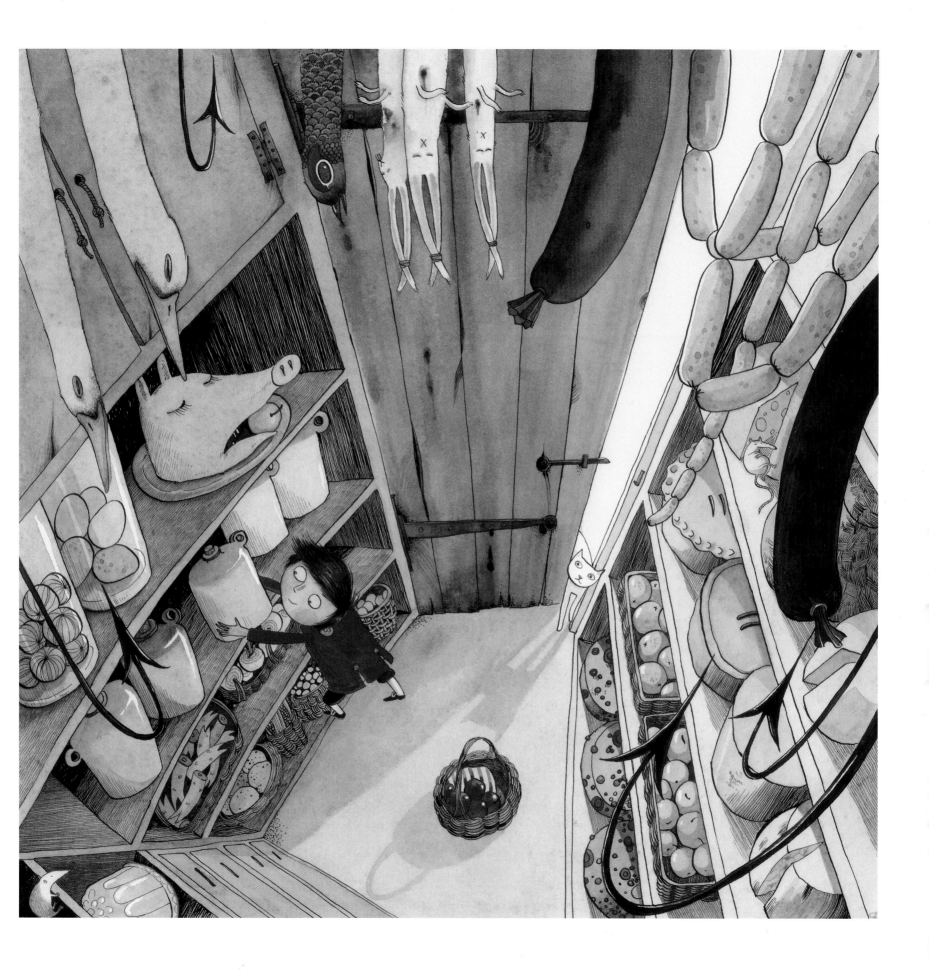

Little Red put on his much-loved red coat, picked up his basket, and set off for Grandma's. As always, his mother warned him, "Don't you wander off the path, not for *any* reason."

Everyone knew that a ferocious and hungry wolf prowled within the forest, and straying from the path would almost certainly mean being eaten!

Little Red skipped along the path, unaware the wolf was secretly watching him. "He would make a tasty snack," the wolf said to himself, drooling at the thought.

Suddenly Little Red stopped and called out excitedly, "Red apples!
I'll have to take some for Grandma."

Overhearing this, the wolf thought, "So Grandma is waiting for him,
is she? Perhaps I can have myself two tasty snacks, instead of just one."

Meanwhile, Little Red was trying to reach the apples. There was a large prickly bush in his way, so to keep his coat from being torn he took it off and placed it on a nearby rock.

This gave the wolf an idea. Grabbing the coat, he charged off at a terrific pace to Grandma's house.

Reaching Grandma's front door, the wolf stopped to squeeze himself into Little Red's coat and knocked on the door.

Grandma, who was very, *very* shortsighted, opened the door, saw the red jacket, and said, "Come right in, Little Red. Why don't we have some ginger ale and a big slice of cake?"

But as soon as her back was turned, the wolf pounced on her, and in one second flat he had swallowed her whole!

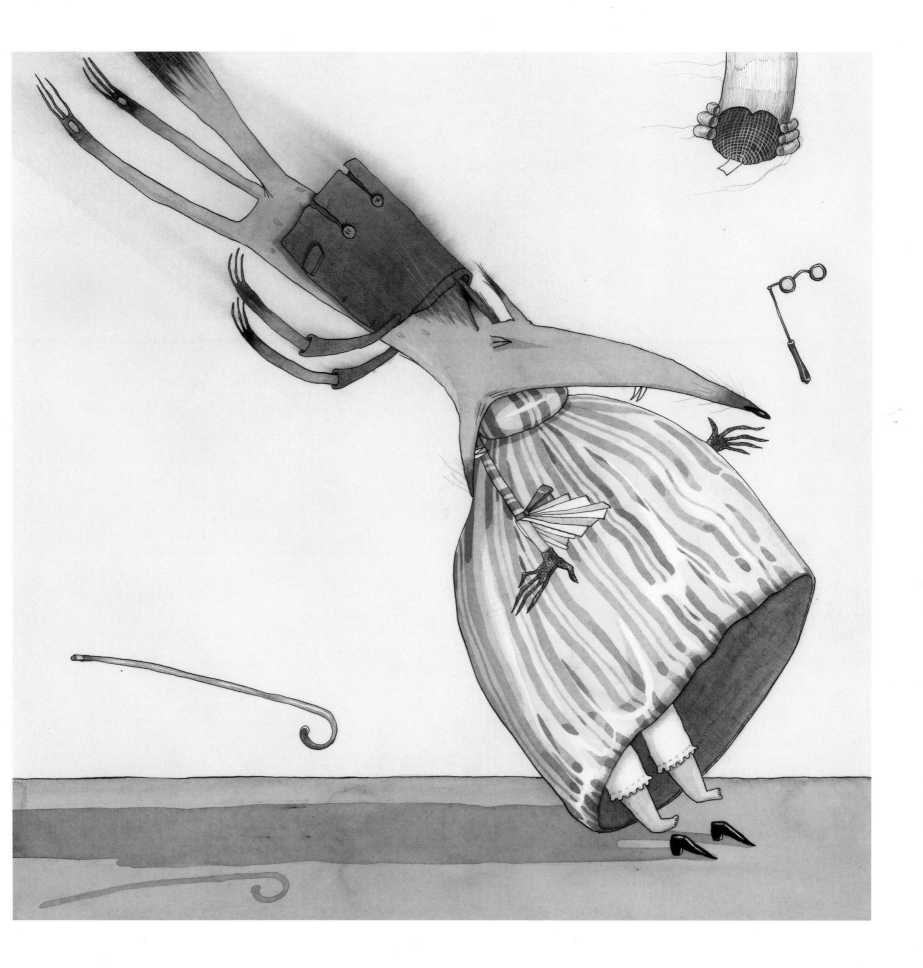

"Now I'll disguise myself as Grandma and I'll eat the boy for dessert," the wolf howled, marveling at his brilliant plan. He stepped into one of Grandma's dresses and fixed one of her wigs behind his long furry ears. He closed the drapes tight, sat at Grandma's table, and waited eagerly for Little Red.

Little Red arrived at Grandma's house out of breath from running.

"Grandma," he cried, "my coat has been stolen! I only left the path for a second, and it disappeared."

When Grandma didn't rush out to greet him, Little Red began to worry. "Are you in there?" he asked, stepping into the darkened room where the wolf sat.

"Grandma," he said, "you look different. Are you feeling unwell?"

"I'm fine, dear," said the wolf sweetly. "Come closer."

"Grandma, what big eyes you've got today," said Little Red, sitting down at the table.

"All the better to see you with, my dear," crooned the wolf.

"But what big ears you have, Grandma," Little Red said.

"All the better to hear you with, my sweet," replied the wolf with a big, toothy grin.

"And, Grandma, what enormous teeth you have!" Little Red exclaimed.

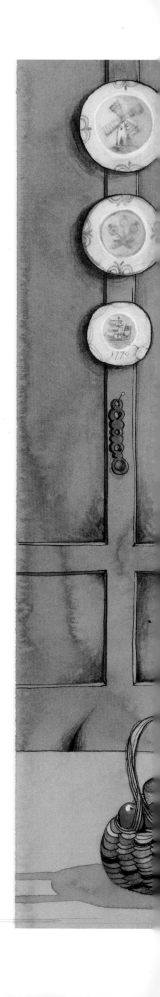

"All the better to eat you with!" roared the wolf.

"What?" cried Little Red. "Don't eat me!"

"You're my dessert," growled the wolf. "Your Grandma was really delicious but not quite enough to fill me up, so you'll finish the meal off nicely."

Terrified, Little Red looked around frantically for a way out. Then he remembered his basket, and had a brilliant idea.

"Wait! I have something much, much tastier than me," shouted Little Red and he grabbed the keg of ginger ale from his basket.

"Tastier than you?" thundered the wolf.

Snatching the bottle from Little Red's hand, the wolf guzzled down the whole thing—enough for an entire week!—in one greedy gulp.

Almost immediately, the wolf's belly began to rumble and grumble loudly.

"Oh dear, oh dear, oh dear," the wolf howled. Then, suddenly, he let out an enormous belch, and out flew Grandma from his mouth!

belch!

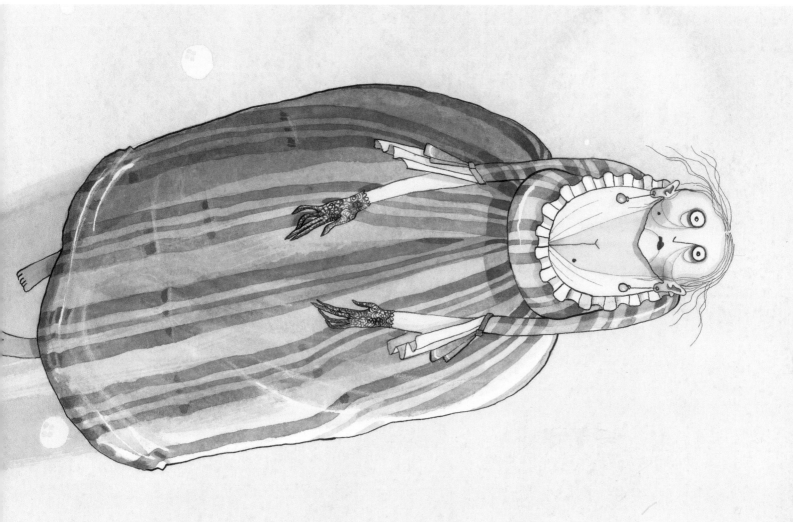

As the wolf tottered backward groaning, Little Red grabbed the empty keg of ginger ale and threw it at the wolf's head, knocking him out cold. Then he quickly tied a pair of Grandma's thick woolly stockings tightly around the wolf's paws.

The wolf awoke with a nasty bump on his head. "My poor, poor head," he moaned. "Eating grandmas is becoming much too dangerous! And that ginger ale was far tastier than Grandma anyway."

That gave Little Red an idea. "If you promise never to eat anyone ever again," he said, "I'll let you go, and make sure you have all the ginger ale you could ever want."

The wolf readily agreed. So from then on, each week on his way to Grandma's, Little Red left a keg of ginger ale in the forest for the wolf, who drank it down eagerly, in spite of its embarrassing aftereffects!

The End

## Illustrator's Note

After exploring the 1930s for our first fairy tale, *Cinderella*, and reminiscing over the 1970s in our second, *Rapunzel*, Lynn and I decided to travel back to the late eighteenth century for *Little Red*, as we wanted this retelling to have a feeling of danger, drama, and suspense. The dark and menacing forest with strange faces in the trees seemed a perfect setting for our sly, scheming wolf to prowl. And the eighteenth-century style of big wigs, satin gowns, beauty spots, powdered faces, and highwaymen fit well alongside it. Ginger ale was a popular colonial drink, and apples were abundant. I researched both European and early American furniture and clothing for this tale, as I envisaged our family to be English pioneers to the new country. Grandma is rather stylish and well to do, and you may recognize a famous painting or two in her house, along with her imported Delft earthenware.
Also, if you look very closely, you will find a couple of links to *Cinderella*!

The illustrations were done in pen and ink with watercolor on hot-pressed, heavyweight paper.

Produced by Breslich & Foss Ltd., London

Designer: Roger Daniels

Library of Congress Cataloging-in-Publication Data:

Roberts, Lynn (Lynn M.)
Little Red / retold by Lynn Roberts ; illustrated
by David Roberts.
p. cm.
Summary: In this version of the Grimm fairy tale, Thomas—who is called
Little Red—discovers a wolf in disguise at his grandmother's house
and ingeniously uses ginger ale to save the day.
ISBN 0-8109-5783-3
[1. Wolves—Fiction. 2. Grandmothers—Fiction. 3. Soft drinks—Fiction. 4. Fairy tales. 5. Humorous stories.]
I. Roberts, David, 1970- ill.
II. Little Red Riding Hood. English. III. Title.

PZ8.R52Li 2005
[E]—dc22

2004029534

Printed and bound in China
10 9 8 7 6 5 4 3 2 1

Harry N. Abrams, Inc.
100 Fifth Avenue
New York, N.Y. 10011
www.abramsbooks.com

Abrams is a subsidiary of
LA MARTINIÈRE
GROUPE

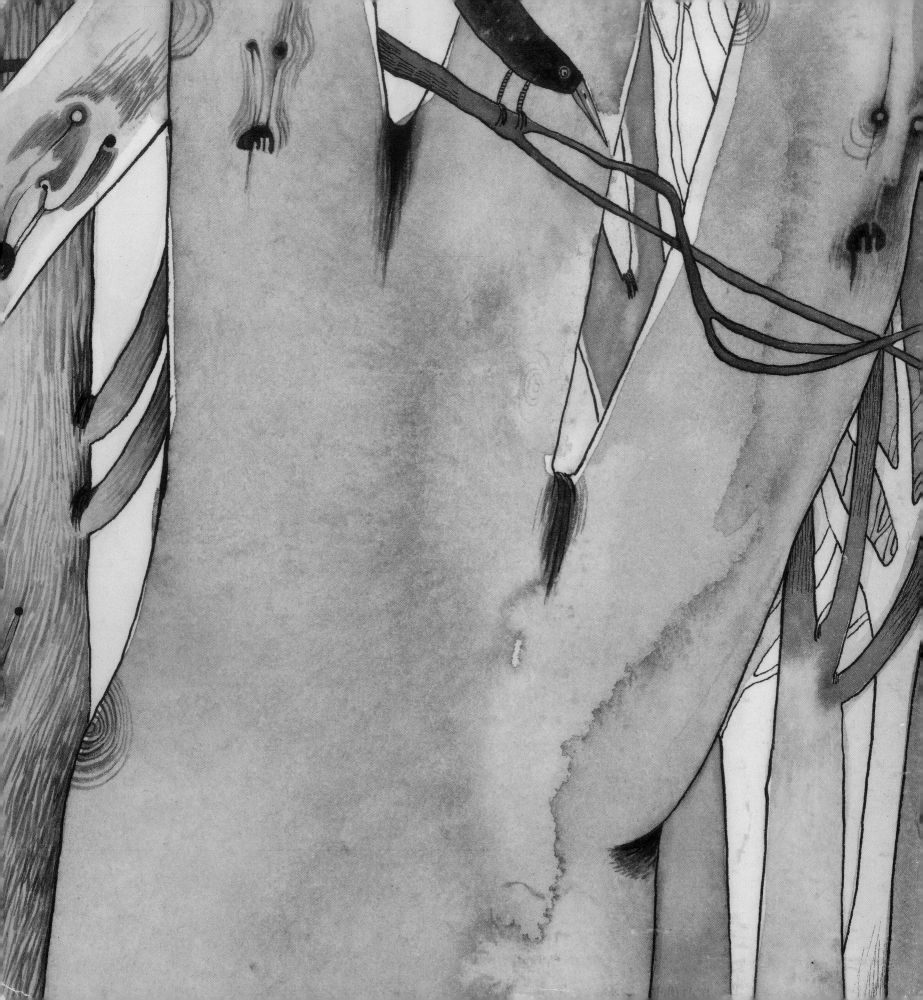